Hansel and Gretel

Text by Maureen Spurgeon

Brown Watson

ENGLAND

Printed and bound in Germany

A MESSAGE TO PARENTS

Reading good books to young children is a crucial factor in a child's psychological and intellectual development. It promotes a mutually warm and satisfying relationship between parent and child and enhances the child's awareness of the world around him. It stimulates the child's imagination and lays a foundation for the development of the skills necessary to support the critical thinking process. In addition, the parent who reads to his child helps him to build vocabulary and other prerequisite skills for the child's own successful reading.

In order to provide parents and children with books which will do these things, Brown Watson has published this series of small books specially designed for young children. These books are factual, fanciful, humorous, questioning and adventurous. A library acquired in this inexpensive way will provide many hours of pleasurable and profitable reading for parents and children.

IN a wooden cabin at the edge of a thick, dark forest, there lived a poor woodcutter and his wife. They had two children – a boy named Hansel, and a girl whose name was Gretel.

Times were very hard, and more often than not, there was barely enough to eat.

"We cannot go on like this, wife!" said the woodcutter, one night.

"And what about the children?" she sobbed. "Suppose we die before they do? Who will look after them?"

"If we leave them in the forest," said the woodcutter, "at least they will have nuts and berries to eat. And noblemen out hunting might find them and give them a home."

Next morning, there was only a crust of bread for the two children to share before they all set out for the forest. Only Gretel saw Hansel putting it into his pocket...

Then Hansel crumbled the bread, ready to drop a piece every few paces as they went through the forest. Now, he thought, they could find their way back home!

After they had gone quite a distance, the woodcutter made a fire to keep the children warm. Stiff and tired, they laid down, hardly caring where they were.

Next thing they knew, it was completely dark!

"We're lost!" Gretel kept crying. "How can we see the pieces of bread to guide us home now, Hansel?"

On and on they walked through the forest, their feet becoming blistered and sore. Suddenly, Hansel stopped. "Look, Gretel! Smoke coming from a chimney!"

It was the ugliest old woman they had ever seen! Gretel turned to run, but the woman spoke kindly.

"Hungry, are we? Come inside, I've plenty of food to spare!"

Suddenly, they heard a voice, cracked and wheezing.

"Who is there? A little mouse?
Who is nibbling at my house?"

"Mmm, delicious!" cried Gretel, picking a leaf. "Try some, Hansel!" But he was already taking bites of sponge cake tiles and wondering if the marzipan roof tasted as good!

Gretel could see nothing. But as they came nearer, the children saw a funny-looking cottage with a pretty little garden, and flowers that sparkled like sugar candy!

Hansel and Gretel had never seen such a meal! How could they have guessed that the kind old woman was really a witch who lay in wait for children?

"A pity they are so thin," she cackled to herself as they slept. "Still, that makes the boy light enough for me to lock him up in my cellar without any trouble!"

Early next morning, Gretel was awoken by a hard kick.

"Get busy, you little wretch!" screamed the witch. "Fetch some water and light the fire!"

Gretel was too frightened to disobey.

"You can cook a meal for your brother," the witch went on. "I want him fattened up before I eat him!"

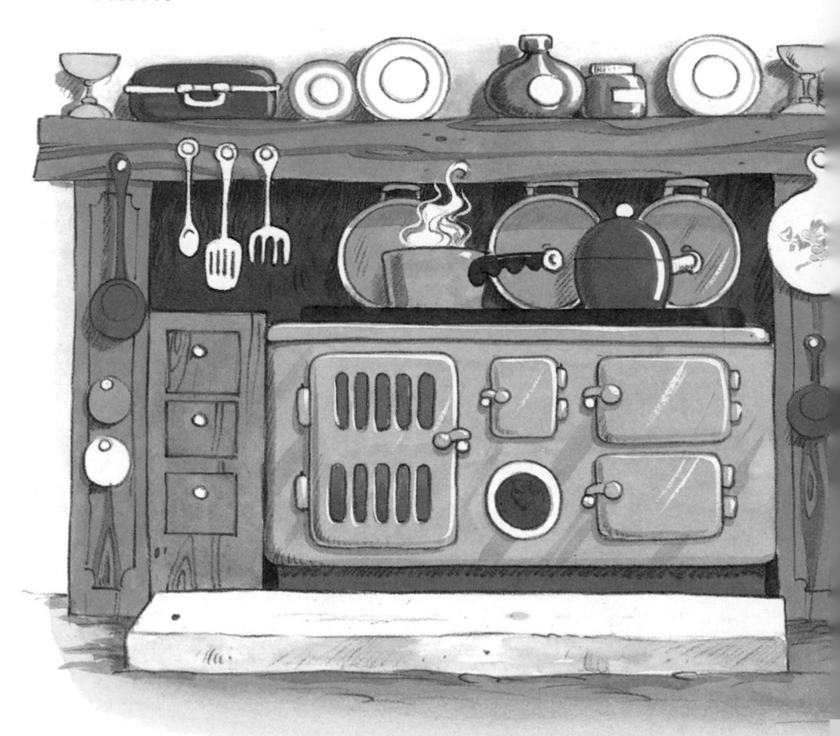

And every day, the witch came to see how fat Hansel was getting.

"Let's feel your arm," she would scream. Hansel always held up one of the bones Gretel passed to him.

Lucky for Hansel, the witch could not see further than the end of her nose.

"Too thin!" she would screech. "Still too thin!"

At last, the witch decided she could wait no longer.

"Girl!" she screamed. "Stoke the fire and get the oven hot! Fat or thin, I mean to eat your brother!"

Hansel was amazed to see Gretel obeying so calmly.

"Please," she said after a while, "will you check to see if the oven is hot enough?"

The witch dashed forward at once, rubbing her hands greedily. And the moment she put her head inside, Gretel pushed as hard as she could – and slammed the door shut!

With trembling fingers, Gretel unbolted the entrance to the cellar.

"Come out, Hansel!" she cried. "The witch cannot harm us, now!"

But Hansel refused to leave the cottage without taking as much of the witch's treasure as they could. They would never need to worry about being cold or hungry again.

How happy they were to hear their mother and father calling them through the forest. They had been searching for the children from the day they had left them.